Apples and Pumpkins

by Anne Rockwell

pictures by Lizzy Rockwell

ALADDIN BOOKS

Macmillan Publishing Company • NEW YORK

Maxwell Macmillan Canada • TORONTO

Maxwell Macmillan International

NEW YORK • OXFORD • SINGAPORE • SYDNEY

For Lucrezia and Ludovica

First Aladdin Books edition 1994
Text copyright © 1989 by Anne Rockwell
Illustrations copyright © 1989 by Lizzy Rockwell

Aladdin Books
Macmillan Publishing Company
866 Third Avenue
New York, NY 10022

Maxwell Macmillan Canada, Inc.
1200 Eglinton Avenue East
Suite 200
Don Mills, Ontario M3C 3N1

Macmillan Publishing Company is part of the
Maxwell Communication Group of Companies.
Printed in Hong Kong
10   9   8   7   6   5   4   3   2   1
The text of this book is set in 24 point Spartan Book.
The illustrations are rendered in pencil and watercolor.

A hardcover edition of *Apples and Pumpkins* is available from
Macmillan Publishing Company.

The Library of Congress has cataloged the hardcover edition as follows:

Rockwell, Anne F.   Apples and pumpkins
by Anne Rockwell; pictures by Lizzy Rockwell. — 1st American ed.
p.   cm.
Summary: In preparation for Halloween night, a family visits Mr. Comstock's farm to pick apples and pumpkins.
ISBN 0-02-777270-5
[1. Halloween—Fiction.   2. Apple—Fiction.   3. Pumpkin—Fiction.]
I. Rockwell, Lizzy, ill.   II. Title.
PZ7.R5943Ap   1989   [E]—dc19   88-22628
ISBN 0-689-71861-6 (Aladdin pbk.)

When red and yellow leaves
are on the trees,

we go to the Comstock Farm

to pick apples and pumpkins.

Mr. Comstock gives us
a bushel basket
to put our apples in.

Geese and chickens
and a big, fat turkey
walk with us
on our way to the orchard
where the apples grow.

My father picks apples.
My mother does, too.

I climb into a little apple tree
and pick the reddest apples of all.

When our basket is full
of red and shiny apples,

we go to the field
where the pumpkins grow.

I look and look
until I find
the best pumpkin of them all.

My father cuts it
from the vine.

I carry it
back to the car.

At home we carve
a jack-o'-lantern face
on our big, orange pumpkin.

We put a candle inside and light it.
Now our pumpkin looks scary
and funny, too.

On Halloween night
we put our pumpkin on the doorstep.
My mother gives away lots of
our red and shiny apples
for trick or treat,

while I go trick-or-treating
up and down our street.